THE COWBOY WAY

COWBOY POETRY—COWGIRL STYLE

BY LISA PAUL

The Cowboy Way: Cowboy Poetry—Cowgirl Style!

Manufactured in the United states of America. Published by:

Double B Publications
4123 N. Longview Avenue
Phoenix, Arizona 85014
(602) 274-7236

Special Thanks to
Al and Mildred Fischer
Phoenix, Arizona
For Editing Assistance

Photographs by
Don Trout
Charlotte, Michigan

Illustrations by
Jim Paul, Sr.
Cave Creek, Arizona

Cover/Book Design & Typesetting
Running Changes
Phoenix, Arizona
(602) 285-1834

ISBN: 0-929-526-66-X

COWGIRL DISCLAIMER:
I was born with a love of animals. As a result, I've endured ringworm, pinworms, the mange and even an occasional flea! I can't imagine what life would be like without a dog on my bed and the cows bawling outside my window. My poetry was created with a deep regard for *the cowboy way* of life. True cowboys and cowgirls do not abuse their stock, through discipline they teach them the way. I could never find humor in cruelty to animals but with a stretch of the imagination I've found humor in life's predicaments. Please enjoy *The Cowboy Way* with this in mind.

DEDICATION

For my husband Jimmie.

Through you I see *the Cowboy Way*. God has challenged us to be strong and with you I have learned that nothing is too difficult to overcome, thank you.

A very special thanks to my father-in-law, Jim Paul.

Your stories and your encouragement have truly inspired me and your illustrations brought my poems to life. Thanks for being a part of my dream.

Lisa Paul ✳

Published by Double B Publications

TABLE O' CONTENTS

THE RIDE

The sun was just up, the mornin' was calm,
   the clank of his spurs echoed down through the barn.
The hard work in trainin' 'ould pay off today,
   (if he can just get around Don's four year old bay).
He knew sorrelly was sure to beat all the best,
   just one awesome horse, to hell with the rest.

The brush swiped the dust that sat fluffed on his back,
   the Show Sheen encouraged his mane to lay flat.
A touch of Corona to dab on the sores,
   on his girth, lips 'n' hocks, to soak in to the pores.
A magnificent tail is brushed from a sock,
   the shimmering hair falls down past the hock.

The fresh smell of Leather New floats through the air,
   as the saddle's slapped on 'n' cinched up with care.
The bit catches sunlight 'n' causes a glare,
   as it's shoved up the mouth 'n' o'er an ear.
Sorrelly looks great (since the welts have gone down),
   from the time he took off 'n' ran near to town.
An' the hair that was rubbed where the hock hobbles strapped,
   can hardly be noticed cuz the hocks are both capped.

The moment to mount is finally at hand,
   if only he'll work as good as he's planned.
A touch of the rein to the right 'n' a cluck,
   his nose dropped down low 'n' his head did a duck.
The perfect smooth motion of spins done just right,
   he feels like he'll really win somethin' tonight.
He races right back with a push of the feet,
   ol' sorrelly feels great "God damn, this is neat!".
The distant roar of the crowd cheerin' on,
   "Must be that good bay that's rode by ol' Don."

The number is called, a deep breath he takes,
   as his chunky red stallion steps through the gates.
So quiet he walks, to the center they go,
   an' as they approach he softly says, "Whoa."

The left lead they take in a circle so wide,
    ol' sorrelly looks perfect with each fluent stride.

Approachin' the middle to then go to slow,
    ol' sorrelly does change 'n' to the right he does go!
"Oh damn! This ain't good, things are goin' ta hell!"
    ol' sorrelly just bumped him up on to the swell!
He's lost his right stirrup 'n' dropped his left rein,
    an' that red horse was causin' his groin to feel pain.

He grabs the right rein (it's all he can do),
    as he gasps a big choke 'n' swallows his chew.
His arms went to flappin' like wings on a bird,
    as sorrelly ran down that long patch o' dirt.
The fence wasn't high, just two rails o' pipe,
    just low enough to clear with one stride.
The problem is this; he's not travelin' straight,
    we hope he can stop. "Someone get the gate!"
"Ferget the gate, he's goin' o'er the top!
    That big sorrell horse isn't wantin' to stop!"

He's holdin' the rein, his horn 'n' his hat,
   if he just had that quirk he could knock an ear flat.
But the fence is a comin', there's pains in his heart,
   as that big sorrell stallion leaped with a fart.
An' o'er he went just like Crocodile did,
   then he jumped one big buck 'n' stopped with a skid.

As the crowd gathered 'round to quietly stare,
   at the trainer that lay there with dirt in his hair,
he finally woke up 'n' said, "Go to hell.
   Where's that damn horse that I'm fixin' to kill?"
Across from the crowd was a big sorrell horse,
   comfortably grazing in an obstacle course.
He rose to his feet 'n' brushed off some dirt,
   as he walked off he limped on a foot that was hurt.

"How much would ya take fer that perty red horse?",
   "How much have ya got?" is the question, of course.
"Don't have much money but what I've got,
   is a nice gentle gelding that won't hardly trot.
Good fer a kid er someone who's old."
   The trainer said, "Great. Consider him sold."

OL' FRIENDS

When I'm old 'n' gray 'n' wrinkled tellin' stories 'round the fire,
    there's one I'm sure I'll tell a lot 'bout a horse we had acquired,
an' a famous cowboy goin' by the name o' J.D. Yates,
    who was known fer wicked ropin' among all the heavyweights.

It was a nippy January at an Arizona show,
    when J.D. caught a glimpse of someone he use to know.
He walked over to say "hello" to a long lost friend named Tom,
    they'd roped together awhile back, he' d wondered where he'd gone.

J.D. got a notion to ask if Tom could rope with him,
    "just fer ol' time's sake?" he asked kindly with a grin.
So he dropped the halter Tom was wearin' 'n' pulled the cinch up tight,
    then proceeded to show up ever' roper ropin' there that night.

See, Tom was one o' them horses that a heeler loved to ride,
    he'd turn in quick 'n' drag his ass when that loop hit jumpin' hide.
So, J.D. walked 'im in the box 'n' pulled 'im gently back,
    then tucked the rein's behind Tom's ears 'n' gave his rope some slack.

I saw the look on the ropers' faces 'n' knew what they were thinkin;
    "J.D.'s gonna kill himself if he don't slow up the drinkin'!"
But that cowboy wasn't drunk, he just had an awesome horse,
    who was the best at heelin' steers (trained by Jimmie Paul, of course).

The chute banged open 'n' the steer ran hard, Tom was on his hip,
    his ears were laid back tight as he ducked 'n' dived with it.
The header stood up high 'n' reached to throw his loop,
    as Tom leaned left 'n' scooted in, the ground drug J.D.'s boot.

J.D. threw a speedy loop that captured jumpin' feet,
    as Tommy drug his big, brown butt, J.D. melted in the seat.
The crowd all went to cheerin', it was really an awesome sight,
    cuz somethin' special happened 'tween two champions on that night.
An' sometimes now I stop to watch ol' Tom turned out to graze,
    an' 'member when he shined so bright back in his glory days.

THE ROCKIN' T

Back when I was a kid' 'round seventeen,
   I was a hand on a ranch outside o' Abilene.
We raised some good horses 'n' I broke the colts,
   I rode wild ones well but I took me some jolts.
There was one colt that always got the best o' me,
   he had a talent fer buckin' that anyone could see.

We had a hell of a time brandin' him. I'll never ferget,
   that rockin' T branded cockeyed on his hip!
Time after time I'd throw the wood on this gray,
   an' he'd dump me in the dirt, day after day.
It was hard on my ego, to say the least,
   but I was downright unable to cover that beast.

They told me I rode 'em good as any champ they'd eyed,
   so I left on a Monday with butterflies inside.
I won me some rodeos, they say I'd earned a reputation,
   fer ridin' the toughest broncs in the nation.

It wasn't long after, my gut calls it fate,
   I had a heck of a draw bangin' chute sevens' gate.
He was a bronc that I knew was respected by all.
   Most cowboys who'd drawn 'im had taken the fall.
I needed to mark high, at least an eighty four,
   if I could hang with 'im eight, I'd get a hell of a score.

I laid my riggin' gently o'er his withers so wide,
   then he growled as the cinch came up tight at his side.
I was told he'd come out high, then duck hard to the right,
   so I sat down real slow 'n' worked my glove in real tight.
I shoved down my hat 'n' nodded real big,
   as he leaped out, my ass left the back o' my rig!
He bucked hard with such force I was thrown to his neck,
   an' I was preparin' myself fer a hell of a wreck!

Only once had I rode one as powerful as this,
   an' I knew I was done as I felt a slip in my fist.
I was thrown high in the air like a cannonball man,
   an' scrambled like a cat who was fixin' to land.

I hit the ground hard, it knocked a lung flat in me,
  an' the lights were all spinnin' as I struggled to see.
I climbed to my wobblin' knees 'n' sat fer a spell,
  thinkin' I'd died, but I couldn't quite tell.

Gray was cornered down at the end o' the pen,
  hoppin' while the flank strap was released by the men.
I noticed that bronc starin' at me like he was lookin' inside,
  an' I got a chill when I saw a rockin'T burned on his hide.

I 'membered a day back not so long ago,
  when I rode ever' horse…'cept one named Lobo.
Fer me 'n' that bronc it was an old familiar scene;
  me layin' in the dirt starin' at a colt that was mean.
I tightened my fist, cuz I knew deep inside,
  I didn't have what it took fer that 8 second ride.
I can't quite explain how I was feelin' right then,
  I had a brand new respect fer that bronc in the pen.

An' I suppose if there was one I wasn't able to tame,
  it's a good thing his picture hangs in Rodeos' Hall O' Fame.

LONESOME OUTLAW

His horse was weak 'n' tired, he'd have to rest tonight,
   he'd need to shade up soon 'n' head out at daylight.
He knew the Federales would soon be on his trail,
   but he couldn't wait on comrades so he busted out o' jail.
He stole a horse at midnight 'n' left that border town,
   before they had him hangin' then eight feet under ground.

He was a wanted man, posters hung in many states.
   Bounty hunters wanted him to pay fer his mistakes.
He knew his days were numbered 'fore he'd own up to his past,
   of shootin' any cowboy who thought his gun was fast.
All he really wanted was to make Laredo 'fore he died,
   to tell the women he loved he was sorry he had lied.

Ever' now 'n' then a man who's livin' life all wrong,
   will have the perfect lady who's strong enough fer holdin' on.
Her name was Larina. She'd lived her ever' night 'n' day,
   waitin' fer the outlaw whom she loved to come her way.
He knew she deserved a man who'd always be there by her side,
   so he told her one dark August night he didn't love her 'n' she cried.

Two long days to Texas with eighteen Federales on his path,
   didn't leave much promise he'd get to take those cruel words back.
What this outlaw didn't know is that this time he wouldn't find,
   Larina in a pretty dress hangin' clothes out on the line.
She'd been gone fer months. They say she simply fell apart,
   an' on her headstone were the words "Died of a broken heart".

This outlaw never made it to that little Texas town,
   the Federales surrounded him that night 'n' shot him down.
He never had another chance to say he loved her er feel her touch,
   an' Larina never heard the truth from the man she loved so much.

PROFILE OF A HORSE TRAINER
(EQUINE ENGINEER)

There's much about trainin' that one wouldn't desire,
　　like colts flippin' o'er 'n' hemorrhoids on fire.
Backs that are achin' 'n' ankles that swell,
　　an' armpits 'n' tube socks that emit a smell.

The arthritis that dwells in the broken finger joints,
　　prevent's the finger from straightenin' when the trainer points.
There's a long dent 'round the skull from wearin' a cowboy hat,
　　it's believed to restrict blood flow to the brain (but not a fact).
The lip that gets a shrivel where the chew sits all day long,
　　gets ignored by tongue 'n' mind cuz not chewin' would seem wrong.

There's corns that grow so hardy along crooked ol' white toes,
　　from boots that push too hard where the circulation flows.
There's calloused grooves along the fingers where the reins do fit,
　　from snatchin' on the horses who are learnin' to respect a bit.
An' knee joints that are pressured on the very outer part,
　　from spurrin' 'round the bellies of horses with no heart.

Trainers can be spotted if they've done it fer any time,
　　cuz they always walk a limpin' (an' never in a straight line).
An' one thing ya know fer sure when yer talkin' 'bout a trainer:
　　If he isn't drinkin' now it means he used to 'n' he quit 'er.
Trainer's pay is minimal compared to all the work,
　　but a cowboy wouldn' work at all if he couldn' taste the dirt.

They never miss a sunrise that would take yer breath away,
　　an' the thunder storms that cool 'em off beats an office any day.
An' the feelin' of a seasoned horse between the reins no doubt,
　　gives a cowboy a special feelin' that most folks don't know about.
There'll never be a college that could teach one in a year,
　　it take's a lot a years o' misery to be an Equine Engineer!

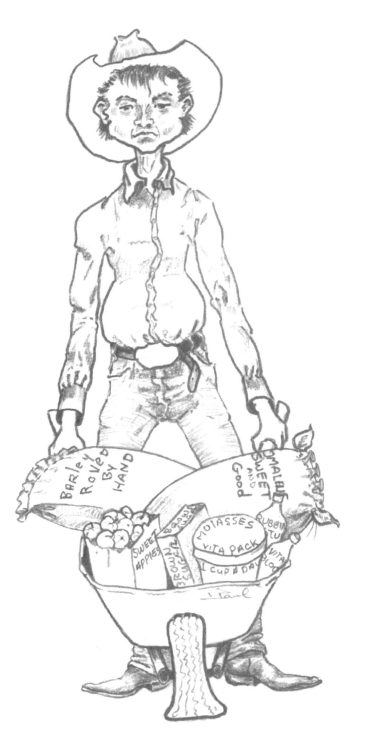

THE CAT FIGHT

He walked with a limp 'n' a wrinkled straw hat,
  he carried a riggin' 'n' a fancy brown bag.
The rowels on his spurs were sharp as cut tin,
   belonged to his dad, he says they helped him win.

He chewed Copenhagen 'n' wore a mustache,
  he was a cowboy who loved buckin' fer cash.
An' cash he did win at most rodeos,
  he rode most the horses to ten second go's.
The cowboys all loved him, they called him The Cat,
   (ever tried pullin' one off o' yer back?)

That must be how them broncs get to feelin',
   with The Cat on their backs 'n' them spurs both a reelin'.
I watched him in Vegas draw one bad beast.
   She'd never been rode 'n' some were down on their knees,
a sayin' a prayer that he wouldn't get hung,
   to the meanest bitch buckin'. Lotsa bells that mare rung.

Her name was Hells' Angel, sent straight from Hell,
   from the Devil who was lookin' fer a cowboy to kill.
Her eyes burned like fire, her ears looked like horns,
   she had bones 'bove her eyes that were pointed like thorns.
Her hide was the color of smoulderin' ash,
   gray, like the faces of the cowboys she'd smashed.
Her mane was as black as burnt ebony,
   she was a tall, chunky mare branded L Lazy P.
She'd tremble in the chute with her head hung down low,
   an' the cowboys'd have to get on her real slow.

I was back 'hind the chutes when The Cat cinched her up,
   an' he talked to her softly as he forced his glove shut.
He moved his spurs forward to mark the wench out,
   an' he shoved down his hat, then he said in a shout,
"Outside, boys!" the gate swung open wide,
   the mare went to spinnin' as The Cat spurred her side.
She'd hang her head low 'n' she'd twist like a bull,
   an' she'd spin 'round 'n' 'round as he'd lay back 'n' pull.

The crowd was a cheerin' 'til The Cat got thrown in,
    to the well that was caused by the force of her spin.
But this seasoned cowboy wasn't 'bout ta quit,
    as he pushed back real hard 'n' sunk deep in his rig.
By the very next jump I was rubbin' my eyes,
    cuz The Cat was straight back spurrin' Hell's Angel's sides!

The crowd was a roarin', thunder rumbled the ground,
    they crowned their new champion in the Finals last round.
The Cat marked 98 in an eight second spell,
    he rode for his life on an angel from hell.
The Devil wouldn't get his cowboy tonight…
    But, even the Devil liked the famous "Cat Fight"!

ROPIN' LESSON

He rode in ridin' tall on his fancy, big red snide,
   an' bragged about his ropin' 'n' how good that he could ride.
Baldy was pretty wicked when turnin' them big steers,
   hell, he oughta be good, a champion roped on him fer years.

Baldy misses pastures since the day this guy showed up,
   with his fancy trailer hooked upon his fancy dually truck.

It happened just like this, on a Sunday hot as hell,
   when we drew up in a drawpot, (he wasn't happy I could tell).

He said a couple rude things as I's pickin' out Brown's shoes,
    "If ya rope like you do usually, we're likely gonna lose."
I ignored the first part, but couldn't get by the last;
    "Ya may wanna borrow Bill's horse, ya'll need one that runs real fast."

I picked up my ol' rope bag 'n' climbed up on my horse,
    said, "I'd hate to break them phony teeth, but will if I get forced".
Nothin' much was said 'til we were backin' in the box,
    he said, "Now 'member, I'm the horns, ya be lookin' at the hocks."
The heat that filled my chest as my blood began to boil,
    caused me to be late 'n' I nearly dropped a coil."

He reached 'n' threw his loop, the steer was runnin' fast,
    he was bounced up pretty high when Baldy kissed his ass.
He just barely got him caught when Baldy did a duck,
    quickly left they went as he said a word that rhymes with duck.
I had a good loop goin' 'n' was sure I'd catch a heel,
    I snagged two feet, dallied hard 'n' heard this grown man squeal.

I looked up, Baldy'd faced 'n' this man was white as snow.
    Then the flagger said, "A finger's gone, hell it looks just like a toe!"
A roper said, "Quick! Give him slack to loosen up his coil!"
    I said, "Heck, it looks as though you're havin' some turmoil."
The cowboys gathered 'round as I had me a little chat,
    with the pansy on the fancy horse wearin' a 40x hat.
His fingers looked like grapes 'n' one was darn sure missin',
    but I wasn't gonna give him slack 'til he did some true ass kissin'.
"Tell me, was the loop that caught two feet the best you've seen?"
    an' he groaned, "Yes...I think so" as he started turnin' green.

Then I asked, "Did yer bald horse outrun my horse Brown?"
    he squelched, "No! Now can you please let me go to town?
I'd really like to see if I can get this sewn back on!",
    then I said, "Don't ya bother, cuz the dog that had it's gone."

Now I don't want fer ya to think about me as an ass,
    but this guy had this comin' from way back in his past.
His braggin' sure did get to us, we'd heard his ever' tale,
    'bout winnin' all the 'big ones' 'n' how his poop don't smell.
I had cowboys buyin' me beers 'n' shakin' off my hand,
    fer teachin' a lesson 'bout ropin' to a man we couldn't stand.

NOT HIS LAST RODEO

A young cowboy from West Texas, he was a combination of,
  his daddy's perseverance and his mamas tender love.
Really just a kid at the age of twenty six,
  when it came to ropin' calves, this kid had some tricks!

He lived to rodeo. The dreams that drove this guy,
  stretched further than that ranch under that big ol' Texas sky.
Branded on his mind were the vivid memories,
  of his mentor's tyin' calves in a fury on their knees.

He watched the tapes of generations in the best of rodeos,
  he learned from watchin' champions rope in their best go's.
They said he had some talent they hadn't seen in quite some time.
  A gentleman from a ranch southeast of the New Mexico line.

Brought up in a Christian home, his values helped him stay,
  the champion all the boys looked up to be some day.
How were we to know his days were numbered few?
  They coulda picked a different rodeo if only they'da knew.

But somewhere on an Oregon night, three cowboys on their way,
  to another rodeo, startin' another short lived day.
A driver that was racin' on what seemed a hellbound flight,
  took the life of one more cowboy on a sultry August night.

In a selfish way we mourn cuz we won't be blessed to see,
  a talented young cowboy become the legend he would be.
Our hearts ache fer the families who have suffered such a loss,
  and fer those who loved the cowboys who rodeo'd at any cost.

I often wonder why we lose our youngest and our best,
  at times it is the one who gave so much to all the rest.
But, I know a lovin' God who will embrace us with his love,
  and watch over Shawn for us while he rodeos with those above.

Shawn McMullan
PRCA CALF ROPER
1969-1996

THE DAY HAROLD LADINK QUIT ROPIN'

Harold called himself a cowboy, he'd claimed it all his life,
    but Harold had some hell, just ya ask his wife.
If anything's to go wrong, it'll be to him.
    (It's probly understandable why he got hooked on gin.)
I've seen some funny things but this one tops 'em all.
    It happened in New Mexico 'n' here's what I recall.

I was watchin' ropers huntin' points fer the World Show.
    Harold rode in bouncin' with his hat pulled way down low.
The show was perty wicked, the best were ropin' there,
    Schroeder, Yates and Wadhams were lined up drinkin' beer.

Harold was an amateur, his header was one of the best,
    (he'd roped with most the others but he'd scared off all the rest).
I could tell he was nervous 'n' that's when things go bad.
    Harold doesn't know good luck cuz bad lucks all he's had.
He fumbled with his rope 'n' backed bay in the box,
    then dropped his tangled coils down by bay's long socks!

He crawled off his big horse but the stirrup hung a boot,
    as Harold's bay horse trotted off it left him hangin' on the chute.
Harold finally got his boot back 'n' his coil's fixed to rope,
    but I could see it in this header's face…he didn't hold much hope.

They finally called their steer, it was one that ran real fast,
    the header caught the horns as Harold ran on past.
Harold took the long way 'round a gettin' to the steer,
    I could tell there was a wreck ahead, my gut filled up with fear.

The roper's waitin' scattered as he came 'round swingin' hard,
    then he threw his big ol' loop 'n' passed the steer by far.
It didn't really surprise me, another one of Harold's deals,
    when I looked up Harold dallied both his header's heels!

This big broad bay he rode was a seasoned ol' rope horse,
    so he planted his broad ass when Harold dallied with some force.
Bay had been around some 'n' knew to get on back,
    so the head horse went on down when the rope ran outa slack.

Harold knew he'd blown it big, then things got a little worse,
   I never knew that header to get mean er ever curse.
That steer then went to ballin' 'n' jumpin' all around,
   an' the bay horse headed south from the chaos on the ground!
It was an awful thing to see; that bay horse pullin' hard,
   a head horse by the heels 'n' a steer back not too far.

If that wasn't bad enough, the header's foot was hung,
   in the stirrup of the head horse that was bein' drug.
Harold was a hangin' on 'n' yellin', "Whoa, now, whoa!",
   but that bay horse wasn't stoppin', it was quite the western show!
Well, ya couldn't hardly blame the horse, thing's had gotten weird,
   I knew trouble was a comin' but it was worse than I had feared.

It took a couple cowboys to get that bay horse caught,
   they got his dally off the horn then Harold took off at a trot.
Not too far behind him was his header on two feet,
   limpin' with one boot off holdin' on to his left cheek.
He screamed, "My ass is killin' me! My horse is hurtin' too.
   An' if I ever get ya in my scopes I'll blow a hole through you!".
Harold never stopped that horse, he headed home a'lopin',
   an' most of us won't soon ferget the day Harold LaDink quit ropin'!

A SILVER CITY NIGHT

In a wild western town back in 1883,
    was a dandy, little brothel run by Kitty McGee.
Up above the best saloon the west had ever seen,
    was a place that ever' cowboy could fulfill his wildest dream.

It was a boomin' town in the heart of the wild, wild west.
    Outlaws, wranglers and gamblers would often stop to rest.
Music played from a piano that pounded out ol' tunes,
    as barmaids took their cowboy guests off to lacey rooms.

Gamblers came from all around to play at Kitty's tables,
    an' listen to the famous outlaws tell their awesome fables.
Bandits were often seen in the windows up above,
    with ladies who had satisfied their selfish need fer love,
watchin' out fer bounty hunters who planned to take 'em in,
    to collect the gold 'er money that the posters promised them.

Tired horses tied along a rusty hitchin' rail,
    pawed up dust from hunger pangs and swished a jaded tail.
Drunken cowboys laughin', one hangin' on the other,
    would fall against the bar and order up another.
The whiskey poured non-stop and ya'd likely see a fight,
    somewhere under a starry sky in a Silver City night.

THE BROWN BOMBER
(AND JIMMIE PAUL)

'Bout once in a lifetime a horse comes yer way,
    that's better than any you've rode in yer day.
That horse came to me when I was twenty-seven,
    I pray they'll have horses like this one in heaven.
He was a rank lookin' three year old, scrawny 'n' lean,
    he was brown with a snip, not the prettiest I'd seen.
But after some time passed he started fillin' out,
    'bout a year down the road he'd grown handsome 'n' stout.

His circles were fancy, he spun like a top,
    an' he slid his brown butt to a country mile stop.
I knew he was special by the time he was four.
    He was doin' four events 'n' he coulda done more.
After all these years he means a lot to me,
    my boys started ridin' him when they were just three.

The side bone 'n' navicular hasn't kept him down,
   he gives a hundred percent when he hits the ground.
Our vet says the surgery won't help anymore,
   cuz the side bone's the evil that's keepin' him sore.
So we bute him 'n' tend him as best as we can,
   an' remember our best horse is now an old man.

His name is Tivio Thomas (Tommy to us).
   This cowy brown gelding has made quite a fuss.
We still go to places where cowboys'll ask,
   "Ya still got that brown horse that always kicked ass?"
See, they called him The Brown Bomber at most of the shows,
   cuz he beat all the best outa most o' their go's!

We won blankets 'n' saddles, money 'n' buckles,
   an' cowboys still ask me with white on their knuckles,
"Are ya plannin' to enter that brown horse ya got?",
   an' I say "Old Tom? Oh…Maybe, maybe not."
Tom can still hold his own, he's gotta heart made o' gold,
   an' it hurts me inside to see Tom gettin' old.

Ya haven't seen nothin' 'til you get to watch,
   ol' Tivio Thomas back in the box.
It takes quite a horse with a big tryin' heart,
   to be feelin' some pain 'n' still do his part.

He's been with me since he's three 'n' he's gettin' up in years,
   I pray he'll be around to teach my boys to rope steers.
Cuz no teacher's better 'bout ropin' them cattle,
   than a campaigner like Tommy. Heck, that's half the battle!

I know one of these days I'll have to say good-bye,
   to the best horse I've rode 'n' I'm darn sure I'll cry.
There's times I say a prayer 'n' tell God I hope,
   that some day in heaven I can catch Tom 'n' rope.

THE COWHORSIN' DELUXE
(The future of western saddlemakers)

If ya ever had it happen where yer teeth yanked out some mane,
    when yer cowhorse turned that hefer like a horse that went insane.
Fer those of ya who've pushed so hard boxin'a chargin' cow,
    yer boot popped through the stirrup 'n' drug ya like a plow.
If things have gotten western when yer travelin' at high speeds,
    on a horse that's runnin' off, switchin' 'n' outa leads.
I've got just the answer but before ya take a look,
    'member not to judge too quick the cover on the book.

It's rightly named The Cowhorsin' Deluxe, but let me say one thing;
    there ain't no reason cutters can't shine upon it in the ring.
This here saddles like no others, the bells 'n' whistles this un has,
    can hold its own to handstamped ones that are cluttered up with snaz.
This un here is functional 'n' that's worth a million bucks,
    it'll pay fer itself the next time ya ride a horse that shys er ducks.
The fenders have a feature with a patented leather flap,
    that you stretch around yer calves with a large commercial snap.
Ya'll never blow a stirrup if the Deluxe is what ya ride,
    cuz each fine cast iron stirrup has a boot welded right inside!

Now let's get to the finer features of this landmark leather piece.
    Notice there's a pair of pants that's lined with fine wool fleece.
Our saddle seats are beautiful, but please take a closer look,
    they're made with velcro plastic 'n' the trick is in the hook.
It's absolutely mandatory you slide yer bottom to 'n' fro,
    so you can get the fleecey pants to stick real hard on the velcro.
Our fine handcrafted saddle seats are like no other kind,
    (but yer required to let the craftsman take a mold of yer behind.)

Notice that the rubber swells are padded to the tips,
    this will minimize the damage from concussion to the hips.
Our patent-pendin' cantle has a built-in spring release,
    to pop ya right back in the seat if the pants rip from the fleece.
We've added one more option that our competitors will hate:
    the leather comes in six bright colors to better help ya coordinate.

If yer concerned 'bout breakin' a cinch, ya can put yer fears to rest,
    cuz there ain't no cinch to break, it's designed by our very best!
All four corners o' the Deluxe strap to the legs o' yer best horse,
    preventin' movement left er right er back 'n' forth o' course!
Now if these features haven't sold ya, ya may as well go back,
    to Rios, Scott er Vancore who makes a primitive type o' tack.

(Fer a limited time only we'll throw the second one in half price,
    but the offers only good TODAY - the boss is feelin' nice.)

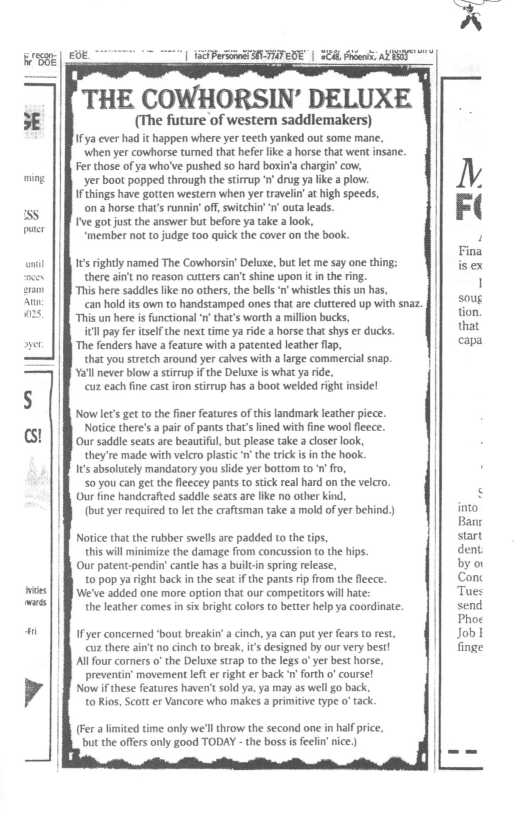

TORNADO'S EYE

They all were up early, the sale was that day,
   best stock in the state was headed their way.
See, calves were a comin' 'n' ever'one knew,
   Hank had it out with his ol' roan named Blue.
Blue changed up his mind 'bout chores on the ranch,
   last trip on ol' Blue left Hank hung in a branch.
It's quite a surprise a horse that fat can buck,
   it starts with a shy, then a jump 'n' a duck.

On back a few weeks ol' Blue lost a shoe,
   an' when Hank went to nail it he swallowed his chew.
His hammer hit one nail, but never the next,
   cuz that fat, chunky roan horse kicked Hank in the chest.
When Festus arrived, Hank lay flat on his back,
   with a shoe in his hand 'n' a dent in his hat.

Hank said, "Gather that roan horse, he'll be in the grain.
   I'll be here with my rope, run him down through the lane!"
Ol' Fest' gathered roany, ran him down through the lane,
   but Hank wasn't watchin' when the rope caught on a chain.
On the chain was a gate that was used as a drag,
   an' the gate took out Hank, knocked him flat on his back!

Festus knew one thing; that horse loved his grain,
   so he headed back down to where roan was last seen.
Then, sure enough, with the dust flyin' high,
   came Roany, the gate and ol' Hank bouncin' by.
Now ya'd think that the man woulda had it by now;
   can't shoe him, can't catch him 'n' he won't work a cow.
But ol' Hank wasn't one to give up on a horse,
   just wouldn't give in ('less he was forced).

Then, one Sunday ol' Hank was forced that's fer sure,
   an' finally decided that horse just ain't "pure".
It happened on down by the north water tank,
   when the roan horse was thirsty 'n' wanted a drink.
Hank slithered off to give Roany a rest,
   he gulped down two gallons 'n' took a long stretch.

Then Hank cinched him up tight to head on down home,
    when that blue beast sucked back 'n' left Hank all alone.

Nine miles from the first gate, four more to the next,
    Hank went to walkin' 'n' hate filled his chest.
He thought of that blue roan that caused him such grief,
    the man who last owned him was a liar 'n' a thief.
Hank didn't mention ol' Blue since that day,
    just that sale at the stockyards on the first day of May.

When they arrived, the horses were penned,
    they wandered around huntin' new stock to tend.
The black one was sore, his right tendon had a puff.
    The bay was a looker but not quite old enough.
The gray needed groceries, "Well, damn, it's a mare",
    her feet were broke up 'n' she needed some care.
"Son of a gun! This brown gelding I see,
    gots a nasty big knot on the front of his knee!"

Then ol' Hank came upon a big emptied pen,
    with a cute lil' geldin' standing down on the end.
He walked on in closer, the geldin' looked up,
    "He seems doggone gentle fer just gettin' off the truck."
His withers were high, but his hip was superb,
    the legs looked damn good ('cept for the curb)."

The hoof showed a crack, probly just dry,
    an' there was a blue spot inside his right eye.
The flank had a strip of hide that was pink,
    not a big deal Hank didn't think.
The hair on the hocks was rubbed off just a tad,
    probly The Itch but it didn't look bad.

Hank sorta liked him, he seemed awful sweet,
    he thought a short horse might be kinda neat.
"He's gotta be better than that ol' blue roan,
    it's time that fat blue horse found a new home."
So Hank took his checkbook 'n' entered the sale.
    One roan down the road, one new horse fer the trail.
And as Hank pulled away feelin' proud of his buy…
    a cowboy waved good-bye to "Tornado's Eye".

GOLDYLOCKS

He was nearly six 'n' dressed the part,
   a silver star pinned on his heart.
The chaps, the boots, the spurs 'n' all,
   a sheriff that stood four feet tall.
Just one thing was missin' in this western show,
   a pony worthy of packin' the sheriff to 'n' fro.
The other one was awful sweet but she had done her time,
   the sheriff had retired her at the age of twenty nine.

"Won't be long" I said to him, "she'll be comin' 'round the bend,
   if she's good as they all tell me she'll be money darn well spent."
We finally heard the bangin' of the trailer pullin' in,
   an' when I opened up the trailer door she kicked me in the shin!
A chunky, yellow pony standin' barely four feet high,
   I noticed right away there weren't no twinkle in her eye.
I told the sheriff to hold on tight, I'd work her in the pen,
   "Don't worry son, she's just Fresh" I said with a big ol' grin.

Her mane was fluffy, it stood straight out,
   her eyes were cranky 'n' she wore a pout.
Her toes toed out, her knees were knocked,
   an' her belly hung down near her hocks.
Her back was swayed 'n' awful long,
   the boy said, "ain't she perty? When can I get on?"

I hitched her on the post real quick,
   'n' watched her as she pitched a fit.
I threw the saddle on her 'n' let the cinch way out,
   then she stepped down on the boot that had the toe that got the gout.
I grabbed her fluffy ankle 'n' lifted her leg up,
   as she reached around real sneaky she nipped me in the butt!

We headed fer the round corral so I could ride her 'round,
   to see if our little sheriff would be safe patrollin' town.
I straddled little Goldylocks 'n' squatted down on her,
   then she darted toward the fence so I hooked her with my spur.
She leaned real hard 'n' rammed me 'gainst the fence with all her might,
   my knee began to swell 'n' my pant leg got real tight.

The saddle started slidin' left as she trotted on around,
   so I leaned way right, a bit too late, as I landed on the ground.
When I hit I noticed my left boot was wedged in tight,
   to the stirrup of the saddle that was draggin' by her side.
It skinned my elbows perty bad, burned a hole through to my shorts,
   she'd drug me durn near twenty feet when my boot jerked off with force.
I'd lost my good straw hat 'bout thirteen feet on back,
   the brim was torn, the band was gone 'n' the crown was kinda flat.

I scrambled to my good knee but couldn't get on my feet,
   when that rotten yella pony kicked me back down on my seat!
I 'membered my granddaddy told me a story 'bout a bear,
   he pretended he was dead 'n' laid real still in fear.
I decided I would try it so I laid myself face down,
   then the boy walked up 'n' said, "hey, what'cha doin' on the ground?"
I lifted my achin' head 'n' rolled o'er on my side,
   as I heard the sheriff say, 'is it time fer me to ride?"

This pony trotted over 'n' sniffed along his shirt,
   as a wilted carrot dropped straight down 'n' landed in the dirt.

He yanked the saddle out from under her belly where it dangled,
    an' worked the twists out of the cinch where it had gotten tangled.
He pulled her nose around as he climbed up in the seat,
    he showed her one limp carrot 'n' she never tried to cheat!

He asked her to go forward 'n' she pinned her short ears back,
    so he wiggled a carrot by her eye 'n' gave her head a whack!
She trotted 'round just fine, never rubbed him on the fence,
    the more I thought about it, the more it all made sense.
He pulled the reins to stop her quick 'n' gave her one more bite,
    heck, the sheriff had her mindin' 'n' she wasn't on the fight!
Then he said, "ya know dad, I've seen ponies in my day,
    that just won't mind 'less ya make 'em think they get their way."

I suppose that Goldylocks 'ould work out on our ranch,
    if the sheriff'll carry carrots in the pockets of his pants.
As I lay there cravin' percocets 'n' feelin' two feet tall,
    I said, "Boy, I can't get up. Could ya give yer ma a call?"

PAYBACKS ARE SWELL

There were times, I must admit, we went a little far,
   in havin' fun at horse shows after drinkin' at the bar.
One sunny afternoon my buddy 'n' I'd had a few,
   we were waitin' on the ropin' class 'n' saw a feller we knew.
He was headed fer the pleasure ring on a fancy yella stud,
   so I grabbed him by the reins 'n' walked him through the mud.
He said, "you guys are assholes" then walked off with a grin,
   then we took a swig of tonic from a bottle filled with gin.

We moseyed on around 'n' grabbed ourselves a spot,
   just in time to see him comin' 'round in a cute lil' trot.
The judge asked fer the lope, the stud was lookin' great,
   but the gin had got the best of us, we were in a jokin' state.
My buddy whispered, "Lookin' good, 'cept yer on the wrong lead",
   he looked at me 'n' said, "Am I really?" as I smiled 'n' agreed.
This guy took it overboard 'n' jerked yeller on his ass,
   as all the other lesser horses slowly loped on past!

Well, my buddy 'n' I knew maybe we had taken things too far,
   so we slithered outa there 'n' back to drinkin' at the bar.
It wasn't long before we heard some talkin' that spread fast,
   'bout a guy lookin' fer two idiots who'd cost him winnin' his class.
"You boys probly think I'm mad cuz ya made an ass o' me,
   but I don't get mad, I get even, as both o' ya will see.
I paid a little visit to yer barn 'n' while I's there,
   I roached the manes o' yer ropin' horses. Now, let me buy ya'll a beer!"

SMOKIN' GUN

It was a hot summer night out on the range,
   it was quiet out there yet somethin' seemed strange.
The fire was cracklin' 'n' the sky was real dark,
   all I could hear was the pound in my heart.
I was countin' the stars in the sky one by one,
   hopin' to sleep 'fore the rise of the sun.

I had two hundred head of wild horses to catch,
   an' one ornery stallion that would soon meet his match.
No one quite knows where he came from,
   legend has it that his name's Smokin' Gun.
My granddaddy told me a story one night,
   'bout the Devil losin' out in a wicked gunfight.

The story tells about a poker game in town,
   all the best gamblers came from all around.
The Devil showed up on a shiny black stallion,
   an' braided in his forelock was a small, gold medallion.
They played fer hours 'n' the Devil lost his stash,
   an' the Gambler asked if he carried more cash.

He removed himself, walked out o' the saloon,
   an' returned with a medallion of a one-quarter moon.
He sat down real slow, slid the gold to the pot,
   said, "My name is Lucifer, in case ya fergot.
An' this is the soul of a cowboy you knew,
   but my gun was faster than his when he drew.

I'd like to offer a proposition tonight,
   that if I lose this hand you'll grant me a gunfight.
If you lose the fight, one more medallion I'll make,
   an' I'll braid it in the mane of my eternal slave."
The Gambler 'cross the table took a whiskey shot,
   an' said, "I know of the gunfight, I loved him a lot."

Legend has it he dealt a good hand,
   four aces won the game fer that lucky man.
So the Devil 'n' the Gambler walked out swingin' doors,
   an' the town quickly lined up in front of the stores.

There was forty feet between 'em, then silence fell,
    an' a warm wind started up from the fires in hell.
Three steps forward then came six loud blasts,
    both fighter's lay still flat on their backs.
Suddenly the stallion reared straight up 'n' broke,
    the rein's that had tied him tight up to the post.

He struck 'n' shook his head, the crowd all moved away,
    as he trotted up to where the Gunfighter lay.
He shoved his nose under him 'n' rolled him on his side,
    when a man suddenly shouted, "My God, he's alive!"
Just then the stallion reared up 'n' pawed in the air,
    then turned 'n' loped away as they watched him disappear.

My grandpa says he knew the man whose soul was saved that day,
    but all the years he was alive he just refused to say.
Tomorrow morn' I'll see this horse 'n' wonder deep inside,
    if there really is a man trapped forever in black hide.

JACK

There's time when a man feels so proud he could crack,
    an' it's pride that's a makin' me tell ya 'bout Jack.
His nose had red freckles, his hair looked like fire.
    He was real close to perfect (Heck, look at his sire!).
He always tagged close on my heels ever'where,
    an' the cowboys 'ould say, "Yer red shadow's still there!".

He'd look up at me with them muddy brown eyes,
    an' I'd give him anything green money buys.
He liked to herd steers, load 'em into the chute,
    I'd bow up with pride 'n' I'd say, "Ain't he cute!".
He liked to ride in the saddle with me,
    so I ordered a new one with a 19-inch seat!

I'd put him to bed in his own ever' night,
    but by dawn ever' day I'd wake up to his sight.
Since he was a baby he's wanted to please,
    it was just yesterday he would bounce on my knees.
It's amazin' how fast my little Jack grew,
    my, oh, my how the past eight years flew!

It's cost me some money to raise him up right,
    I've taught him some manners but if he's cornered he'll fight.
He knows when to push me 'n' when to back off,
    all I have to say is, "Now, Jack, that's enough!"

There's cowboys who ask me if I'd like one more,
    like my little, red Jack 'n' I say, "What for?
With a heeler this good who needs one more dog?
    Besides, he costs me a fortune 'n' he eats like a hog."

POCO'S DELITE...AND IKE

Ever had a memory go through yer mind,
   when ya burst out a laughin' 'n' go back in time,
to a somethin' that happened that just was too great,
   to ever ferget about? Can ya relate?

That very thing happened to me yesterday,
   as I 'membered a memory that won't go away.
It's 'bout a black horse named Poco's Delite.
   Delight he was not, he was black as the night.
His eyes were them small ones, empty 'n' cold,
   he was broad as a barn door, man was he bold.

See, there was this kid from northern Utah,
   who needed a job 'n' I knew his pa.
So I hired him on, not much of a hand,
   but he'd work awful hard, nice kid...understand?
He wanted to learn, so I taught him some things,
   'bout bendin' 'n' softenin', 'bout snaffle's 'n' ring's.
Told him 'bout tie down's 'n' dallie's 'n' such,
   'bout draw rein's 'n' martingales 'n' drivin' one up.

When Poco's Delite was delivered that day,
   he jumped outa that trailer 'n' we jumped outa his way.
He blew out a snortin' 'n' pawin' the ground,
   I said to the lady, "Best go back to town.".
Cuz a battle was comin' with this S.O.B.,
   an' it wasn't a sight fer a lady to see.
Well, I knew of his kind, I'd seen 'em a lot,
   an' they'll fight 'til they're bloody. They'll strike 'n' blow snot.

The kid was real nervous 'bout leadin' the horse,
   so I said, "Cowboy up", (politely, of course).
The kid never did wanna do things like that,
   so I smiled real nice 'n' gave him a pat.
Said, "Get that horse saddled 'n' on over here.",
   as I gathered my rope, a whip 'n' a beer.
Then I heard a commotion that rattled the barn,
   an' I saw that the black horse had Ike by the arm.

He said, "Make 'im let go. It's hurtin' a bit!",
   so I walked up 'n' gave that spoiled horse a swift kick.
I saddled 'im quick 'n' grabbed all my tack,
   'fore that sorry black horse had a chance to set back.

The way to the square pen was tryin' fer sure,
   cuz that horse kept a steppin' on the back o' my spur.
So I'd stomp on his ankles 'n' snatch 'im on back,
   an' he'd rear in the air 'n' he'd strike at my hat.
We entered the pen, put the chain on the gates,
   an' I tied the reins back to my busted up Crates.

I said to the kid, "Do you member when,
   I taught you to work a horse in this pen?".
He said, "I sure do, but you go on ahead,
   I'm afraid if I work 'im I might end up dead."
I said, "Boy, get on in here! Work 'im just like the rest,"
   an' walked outa there, put the boy to the test.

I walked in the barn, just out o' sight,
   an' peered through a stall at that horse black as night.
The kid took the rope, thread it through the chin strap,
   went around Blackie's neck 'n' then pulled down his cap.
He knelt down 'n' slowly reached fer the whip,
   as that burly, black gelding did a jump, then a kick.

He just missed Ike's head, knocked his cap to the ground,
   then that horse went to buckin' around 'n' around!
The rope that had laid at that kid's shakin' feet,
   was now once 'round the post 'n' back 'hind his knee.
When Blackie bucked forward it tightened the rope,
   an' it drug that poor kid right up to the post!

I was hopin' that black horse wouldn't do what he did,
   as he bucked 'round the post wrappin' rope 'round the kid.
Each time he went 'round that post 'n' that kid,
   that ole rope got more short 'n' that kid got more red.
In no time that black horse ran outa rope,
   an' that kid 'n' that horse were left nose to nose!

Neither could move, the rope was too tight,
   an' I couldn't believe that incredible sight!
This big, nasty black horse named Poco's Delite,
   was starin' right into the eyes o' poor Ike!
I stood there a moment 'n' thought what to do,
   then a thought came to mind at a quarter to two.

I decided to leave 'em to soak in that state,
   so I left 'em right there 'n' checked 'em 'bout eight.
He said, "Yer not gonna leave with this horse in my face,
   I'm a bit claustrophobic 'n' I'm needin' some space!".
I said to the kid with the horse at his chin,
   "I'll bet ya won't work one so sloppy again.
I'd guess 'bout eight it'll start to soak in,
   that ya must coil yer rope 'fore ya begin.

An' as fer that black horse that's roped to yer knees,
   he ain't comin' off that post 'til them eyes both say please.
So ya may as well try 'n' catch yerself a nap,
   although it might be a lil' tryin' with that beast in yer lap."

I moseyed around doin' chores fer six hours,
   clipped horses, cleaned saddles, even planted some flowers.
It was awful tough not to laugh when I'd see,
   that big, black, bold horse roped at the knee,
with his nose in the face of that kid we called Ike.
   To this day I still smile when I 'member the sight!

PROFILE OF A FARRIER
(EQUINE SHOE SALESMAN)

I'm pertin' near fifty 'n' shoein's my game,
  been doin' fer years 'n' my back ain't the same.
I've lost a few nails (off my fingers, that is),
  an' I've broke a few rasps on quite a few ribs.
I've had me some heck that nobody knows,
  ('cept the ones who might notice I'm sportin' eight toes).

When I was a kid, 'fore I knew much about shoein',
  I was poundin' a shoe, intent on what I's doin',
when a big, buckskin stud bit off my right ear,
  he was a pricey, big halter horse, but I didn't care.
I took my stand 'n' hit him right side the head,
  I was quite disappointed when I was told, "He ain't dead".
I'm afraid I'd have to say he got the best o' me,
  cuz small ears are the highlight in my family tree.

The hairs in my nose tend to itch quite a lot,
  from smellin' the smoke from the shoe when it's hot.
All o' my hat's got dark rings 'round the crown,
  from the sweat drippin' up when I'm bent upside down.
My dentist tells me I gotta deep groove,
  on the edge of my teeth that he's wantin' to smooth,
from grittin' the nails in the front good 'n' tight,
  as I'm holdin' the hoof of a horse on the fight.

My wife got twin beds, can't stand the pain,
  'tween my sandpaper fingers 'n' my toenails that hang.
I can no longer walk straight er travel real fast,
  since an Arab hauled off 'n' kicked me in the ass.
I bought me a back brace, it holds my beerbelly in,
  so I can see 'round my gut as I pound the nails in.

An' the owners inform me what shoes'll work the best,
  then stand around me supervisin' 'til the completion of my test.
One time there are sliders needed, "with a trailer kinda short,"
  the next time it's, "He still don't stop! Yer fired!" they report.

Er maybe it's the wedges they want wedged a smidgin' more,
  so I offer them advice (that they continue to ignore).

An' often times I get the blame fer somethin' nature'd done,
  in creatin' a wavy, narrow hoof on a sorry, crippled one.
An' damned if any o' my shoes should come loose er fall apart,
  "I'll shoot that lousy farrier point blank right through the heart!"
Er worse they do stay on but a horse steps down just right,
  an' tears a chunk o' good wall off as the shoe sinks outa sight!

I'd often like to speak my mind when I've had all that I can stand,
  an' tell 'em their little, poopsy pony needs ta fill an Alpo can.
I could be chargin' more I guess, but it's a livin' don't ya know,
  an' there'd be no time fer shoein' horses if I had a wad to blow.
So, 'spite me havin' hell, I'll keep doin' this thing I do,
  an' hope them damn computers don't learn to build a shoe!

THE COWHORSE ANONYMOUS

I brushed my teeth 'n' rinsed real well,
　　then neurotically filed a broken nail.
I climbed in to bed 'n' stared at the ceilin',
　　tryin' to ignore that horrified feelin'.

Ya know the one…just 'fore a show,
　　when ya imagine the worst would occur in yer go?
Like, what if her new hat doesn't stay "glued",
　　an' flies off 'n' lands where the hefer just pooed?
How 'bout if yer chasin' yer cow down the fence,
　　an' yer saddle slides off from a break at the cinch?

Er people start starin' cuz yer show shirt is torn,
    then while workin' a cow yer bra snags the horn!
What if yer horse takes a hold of the bit,
    an' lunges ya outa the seat where ya sit?
Nothin' much worse when yer horse makes a cut,
    an' yer jerked back real hard an' yer head hits his butt.
Ever slowly slide off 'n' pretend ya were hurt,
    to look fer the diamond off yer ear in the dirt?

He might spin real fast 'n' cause quite a wreck,
    as the well sucks ya in 'n' ya hang from his neck!
What if the zipper on yer favorite chaps breaks,
    an' each stride they flop up 'n' cover yer face!
Then maybe a snap on yer rein wasn't tight,
    an' came off down the fence…what a horrible sight!
The humiliation sinks in deep as yer walkin' outa there,
    with mat's 'n' sweat 'n' bobbypins danglin' off yer hair.

Oh, the tossin' 'n' turnin' 'n' flaylin' in bed,
    cause the sheets ta get tangled up over my head.
Then I sit straight up with my eyes open wide,
    as I breathe hard I grasp at the ache at my side.
I've practiced 'n' practiced on workin' the cow.

So, do I circle up first? Oh, I can't recall now!
It escapes me 'bout stoppin'! What do I do with the reins?
    Do I push 'em er pull 'em? (As my gut gurgles pains.)

The strain o' the vision o' things goin' bad,
    is worse than the gallstones I recently had.
The absence of sleep has left me quite ill,
    so I decide to gulp down just one sleepin' pill.
It helped me relax, I slept near to One,
    an' awoke in a sweat from the afternoon sun!

I yanked back the sheets, stubbed my toe on the frame,
    an' frantically tried hard to think with my brain.
I gathered some clothes up, slipped my boots on my feet,
    then laid on the horn as I weaved down the street.
I skid into the showgrounds, sideways to a stop.
    Dust engulfed my trainer who sipped on a pop.

I jumped out 'n' grabbed him, I shook him real hard,
    "Tell me now quick! When does my class start?"
He said, "Yer too late, it was over by noon."
    As I stood there in jammies with stars 'n' a moon.
My hair was a rat's nest, my flannels were hot,
    an' I had a powerful cravin' fer a Crown Royal shot.

As my boots flopped I staggered bugeyed to my car,
    I was headed fer the first stool at the nearest dive bar.
I had to do somethin', but my plan wasn't clear,
    there was only two weeks 'fore the next show was here.
Then I picked up my cell phone 'n' talked in it real low,
    "Cowhorse Anonymous? I need a meetin' to go to 'fore my
    next show".

A COWBOY WE CALL "RED"

He was born to rope 'n' rodeo, I see it in his eyes,
 ever' time he swings his loop, I can see how hard he tries.
A cowboy in the makin' at the tender age o' two,
 he insists on doin' ever'thing he sees the big guys do.
Reachin' in a wrangler pocket fer an invisible nip o' chew.
 He pretends he's spittin' in an empty can o' Mountain Dew.

He practices the routine of a cowboy ropin' a steer,
 he backs Stick in the box, nods, then whips him in the rear.
They trail a hard runnin' steer as fast as boots can run,
 when Stick get's rank 'n' bucks 'im off, it makes it much more fun!
Swingin' a practice rope was mastered months ago by Red,
 so don't insult him by handin' him one, he'll take a Classic instead.
Chinks are needed often to help a cowboy grip a thigh,
 of a world champion buckin' bull that's connected to a guy.

There's hardly an ounce o' fear inside this little buckaroo,
 he knows there's always been someone who'll help a cowboy o' two.
But ever' now 'n' then a bloody scrape 'er a stranger's scold,
 will send this little cowboy stampedin' in tears fer a mama to hold.
An' it's often said at nighttime to a cowboy we call "Red",
 "Sometimes cowboys suck on thumbs 'n' drag a blankie off to bed."

ONE LONELY COWBOY

The Cowboy Way is all I've ever known,
    ranchin' 'n' horses was a way of life at our home.
My daddy once told me ya gotta be tough,
    to live this way of life can be pretty rough.
There's more work for one man most days on this place,
    but I wouldn't trade it fer nothin' I need wide open space.

I love takin' my pole where the fish are so thick,
    ya can't see the bottom of that tricklin' crick.
The cattle, the horses, the smell of fresh hay,
    make me thank God I'm here livin' this way.

My grandpa'd be proud to know I still have this ranch,
    my daddy was born in that house that still stands.
Along on the mantle are memories so sweet,
    of the days when I rodeo'd. I hardly got beat.
The pictures have faded, the whites are now tan,
    of me 'n' my daddy, my number one fan.

There's times I have a need to hold the brands on the wall,
    an' remember the times they were held by my pa.
Somedays when I'm restin' my feet on the porch,
    I hear a bang at the barn from the wind on a door,
an' I imagine my daddy shoein' his bay.
    The shoes that he built were the best, people say.

An' when I was a boy I'd hide in the loft,
    from my mom who called out in her voice sweet 'n' soft.
Some nights as I lay in my bed after dark,
    I can still hear her singin' 'n' a pain fills my heart.
Mama's garden grew sweet melons 'n' tomatoes so red,
    those vines she once planted still grow in that bed.

Ever' summer 'bout June when the warm winds would come,
    the water tank would heat from the rays of the sun.
An' me 'n' my heeler would swim until dark,
    'til mama would call us from the gate in the yard.
I buried my blue dog by that tank one sad May,
    an' that faded white cross breaks my heart to this day.

See, this ranch isn't fences, cattle 'n' land,
    it's the memories of our family 'n' the life my dad planned.
So pa, if yer listenin', please tell the rest,
    that I still have the ranch 'n' I'm doin' my best.
An' God can ya help me keep up with the chores,
    'til yer Guardian Angels lead me through Heaven's doors.

THE KID

We gathered our popcorn, a program 'n' a beer,
   then we hustled through the crowd fer the event of the year.
When it came to ridin' bulls, I liked The Kid.
   He thrilled the fans with the stunts that he did.

A scrawny, young cowboy who was hardly drinkin' age,
   'ould toy with them bulls 'til they were hookin' with rage.
Ya'd think them eight seconds 'ould take it outa him,
   but if a bull's on the hook he liked toyin' with 'em.

That night he drew Fat Albert, a bull that no way,
   fit the nice guy cartoon. He'd hooked some good ones they say.
A chocolate brown beefmaster who'd blow snot 'n' growl,
   he'd jump high like a dolphin 'n' strike hard at yer rowel.
He'd been rode only once, The Kid had marked 94.
   He was bound 'n' determined to ride him once more.

This cowboy took his time, he knew it had to be right,
   he wasn't in the mood to get bucked off tonight.
He had carefully laid the back of his hand flat,
   an' continued the routine of a suicide wrap.

He pushed down his hat 'n' said a prayer lookin' up,
   then said, "let 'er rip" as Fat Al spun out left with a duck.
The Kid rode him hard rakin' Fat Albert's side,
   each high jump he took The Kid spurred more hide.
Then Fat Albert did what Fat Al does best;
   stopped hard on the front, his head hit The Kid's chest.

He took the blow hard, it knocked him off o' Al's back,
   but The Kid was hung floppin' to that suicide wrap.
The crowd was all gaspin', the clowns were workin' hard,
   but Fat Al wouldn't let 'em near The Kid's arm.
Then The Kid figured the only way outa this,
   'ould be gettin' back on 'fore he hurt his good wrist.
So he got to his feet then pulled himself on,
   an' Fat Al quit buckin' cuz the flank strap was gone.

We watched as The Kid rode this bull 'round the pen,
    long trottin' lookin' fer a gate to go in.
He quickly worked his glove outa that wicked wrap,
    then reached back 'n' gave Fat Al's bottom a pat!
The crowd was all standin', cheerin' at the sight,
    of The Kid trottin' on Fat Al who was plum outa fight!
I thought I'd seen it all through the years o' my past,
    but I can't recall a bullrider pattin' a bounty bull's ass!

TAKE CARE O' PARDNER

I found 'im layin' there in the snow, icicles glistenin' through his mane,
an' my eyes welled up with tears 'n' my gut twisted up with pain.
I tipped off my ol' cowboy hat 'n' then sunk down on my knees,
I bowed my head to pray 'n' said, "God, hear me, would ya please?
I knew ya'd come 'n' take 'im soon, he'd lived a good long life,
an' I know he's in good hands Lord, but it cuts me like a knife.

I don't wanna be no trouble, but can I ask a favor of ya today?
Could ya grain 'im in the evenin's? Just half a can I'd say.
An' he grows a real long forelock 'n' I'd like fer him to see,
the greenest mountains 'n' alfalfa fields. Could ya trim 'em up fer me?
He always loved them cattle, so I turned 'im out with 'em to graze,
right here in this pasture where his quiet body lays.
So would it be too much to ask, if ya could gather up a few,
so he can buck 'n' play 'n' chase 'em just like he used to do?

An' he always had an itchy spot, fer whatever that it's worth,
if yer Angels get some time Lord it's a spot along his girth.
I never let 'im go too long without brushin' through his tail,
(ah…never mind. I'm sure all them cocklebur patches er in hell).
I know ya ain't seen me much in church 'n' I've done a thing er two,
that didn't make ya proud I'll bet, but I promise this to you:

I'll try to do the things I know are right deep in my heart,
an' things I ain't been doin'…well, I promise that I'll start.
Please take care o' my ol' friend 'til I can call 'im in someday,
an' thank ya Lord fer listenin'. I do love this ol' blood bay.
Oh, an' one more thing I'd like to ask before I let ya go…
could ya tell my buddy he's welcome to take 'im to a ropin' er rodeo?"

Goodbye ol' friend, I'll miss ya lots. You take care, ya hear?
I'll be right behind ya pardner 'n' I'll bring my cowboy gear.

MAMA'S CHORE'S

There's a whole lot o' chores fer a mama of two,
   besides dishes 'n' laundry 'n' cleanin' to do.
Like bucklin' on holsters with guns on two boys,
   who are off to fight Indians with the utmost of noise.
An' threadin' little chaps through Wrangler belt loops,
   while the other loads the bull into imaginary chutes.

Heck breaks loose when a dent gets bumped into a hat,
   tears that drip on dirty boots 'til it's fixed 'n' given back.
There's reins that keep on breakin' on the very best dun horse,
   that travels 'round the house mounted on a stick, of course.
An' the lace ups that the little one can't seem to figure out,
   keep mama on her knees while little boots kick all about.

Then the coils 'n' the loop that get thrown upon the ground,
   need fixin' immediately as the redhead stomps around.
The wrappers from the candy hid so secretly away,
   lay scattered by the purse where it was hid fer treats someday.
An' the pillow cases used as capes so Superman can fly,
   are dropped careless on the floor just after rescuing a guy.

There's rodeos that run each night upon a mother's knee,
   with buckin' broncs 'n' bulls the cheerin' crowd looks on to see.
Bubbles that need poured to hide the sharks deep in the tub,
   that the cowboys fight with horses that are led by Captain Mud.
The shovin' matches always need a referee nearby,
   to interrupt the low blow either one is sure to try.
An' saddlin's not easy fer two boys that just can't reach,
   the withers of the pony mama saddles on her knees.

It's funny how a mama's chores don't ever seem to end,
   but soon two little bandits will be big fer pitchin' in.
Until then she kisses cheeks 'n' wipes a runny nose,
   an' somewhere close to midnight…off to bed she goes.

THE R.O.P.I.N.' SYNDROME
(REGRESSIVE OBSTRUCTIVE PARENTAL INAPT NEUROSIS)

He's a cowboy made o' steel, confident in ever' move.
 He's won a chest o' buckles so there's nothin' left to prove.
Young eyes lock on his movements, they want to rope like him,
 so they pay utmost attention while they're in the practice pen.

His glove guides floatin' loops that gather up draggin' feet,
 (fer sure the kinda heeler any header'd like to meet).
Smooth handles at the corner, no steers jerked through the turn,
 his children watch him carefully, absorbin' all that they can learn.

But somethin' funny happens at youth qualifyin' shows,
 er when he's backin' in the box at all the junior rodeos.
They say it is a "Syndrome" that describes a list o' ails,
 includin' cotton mouth 'n' chewed off, bleedin' fingernails.

Patients report restrictions in the throat caused from a lump,
 an' ropes that feel like cables 'n' a heart that skips a thump.
An' some will say their vision blurrs when they back into the box,
 an' their ropin' hand goes numb 'n' their elbow sometimes locks.

There was one case in the final round, a dad broke down 'n' cried.
 (The embarrassment he must of felt with grown men at his side.)
Occasionally a Champion will succumb to this strange ill.
 Sad there ain't no cure, no treatment er no pill.
They simply have to tolerate the symptoms that they get,
 ever' time they enter up with any motivated kid.

Nausea, sweats 'n' swollen tongues are all reasons fer concern,
 ever' fathers pre-disposed, at any time a dad could turn.
So it's important that one pay attention 'n' watch a father close,
 for symptoms that could surface durin' one o' his ropin' go's.
There really isn't much a carin' soul can do…
 although, they say a shot o' whiskey can sometimes help 'em through.

It's surely aggravatin' when a competent cowboy chokes,
 it's not easy on the kids who think the world o' their folks.
So, if ya want yer kids to rodeo ya'll have to find a way,

to bite yer lip if yer tongue has somethin' sharp to say.
There is one other option fer the mom who feels the strain,
    ever' time her children lose out cuz her husband lost his brain.
Gather up some ropes 'n' a good rope horse to ride,
    an' practice, practice, practice so yer ready to rope if ya decide.
But, one thing I'll have to warn ya 'bout before ya get too bold,
    there are women who can get this thing, I've recently been told.
So it's really in yer best interest to let a sleepin' dog just lie,
    make excuses fer his ropin' 'n' be sure to say "nice try".

(Do it fer the children, if fer no better reason,
    so they can try to finish qualifyin' 'fore the completion of the season!)

EXPERT TIPS ON BUYIN' A HORSE

Color is least on the list o' details (however, bays seem to do real well),
  an' the bluebook price is up a bit if they sport a mane 'n' tail.
They say you'd best stear clear o' chromy ones with three or four
  socks, an' never buy a horse, they say, with white above his hocks.
A hoof that's not jet black is prone to problems, I've heard 'em say,
  an' you'll never get an athlete if his back has got a sway.

The closer both the eyes are to one another tells alot,
  (this scientifically reveals if there's intelligence er not).
An' never, never buy one that's got white up 'round his eye,
  he'll likely get infections, conjunctivitis er a sty.
Look closely at the cannon bones, ya don't want 'im to be tall,
  it's best if they're made short 'n' thick (at least, that's what I recall).

Don't buy one with a bridle path cuz he wasn't ridden by a hand,
  (that's what the experts say, but I'm not sure I understand).
Hooves should be round like eatin' plates, the farriers all boast,
  (but do they mean the salad ones? Er the one used ta cut yer roast?)
Don't trust the one that shows some white when he's lookin' straight
  ahead, them er said to be the ones that most the trainers dread.

It's not a bad idea to see how many owners owned a horse,
  if it exceeds ten in two years ya'll wanna pass, o' course.
The list o' attributes that I've recorded o'er the years,
  usin' tips from expert cowboys has left me broke 'n' near to tears.
See, 'bout four long years ago I had a chunk o' change to spend,
  on a dandy lil cuttin' horse that might win some in the pen.

If it wasn't fer this wrinkled list I've held in sweaty hands,
  I woulda bought a horse years ago 'n' wrapped up all my plans.
But, ever time I find one that I know is quite a "steal",
  he's got a bridle path er three white socks 'n' it blows the shittin' deal!
I've been more than patient kickin' tires 'n' I've had a belly full,
  o' them "experts" who have fed me this long list o' cockin' bull!

What the airplane tickets, rental cars 'n' hotel rooms has cost,
   leaves me with $1,200.00 ($14,000.'s what I've lost).
I'd like to hand the balance to a cowboy who "knows his stuff",
   an' bust his teeth the second he says $1,200.00 ain't enough.

WILD ANGELS

A worn out saddle 'n' a campfire was home to us back then,
    This story I'm fixin' to tell ya's good, but where do I begin?
It was february, eighteen eighty one, it was a cold 'n' blustery day.
    Destination Spearfish. We'd lost two men along the way.
A northern front moved in 'n' caught us up along a ridge,
    we headed fer two canyon walls that held a broken bridge.

Pushin' five hundred head o' cattle with four hours left to burn,
    the only place to cross the river wasn't lookin' worth a durn.
The winds in the mouth o' the canyon blew cold as a witches' tit,
    an' I knew we'd be hardpressed to get any soakin' timber lit.
Our foreman hollered, "Turn 'em back, we'll lose 'em all if we cross here!",
    but the cattle, they weren't listenin', as they jumped in steer by steer.

The roarin' o' the whitecaps sent chills along my spine,
    as I whipped ol' Sorrelly closer I tried to cut 'em out o' line.
The rain hit hard along my brim, Sorrelly trembled 'tween my knees,
    my soakin' glove kept swingin' the rope that was tryin' hard to freeze.
Up the banks, through roarin' rain, I heard the frantic yellin' of men,
    as one by one we lost our herd, the rivers waters rose again.

The current grabbed at Sorrelly's legs as he lunged to get away,
    but the river won the battle we were destined to fight that day.
The bubblin' waters overcame us but I never lost the rein,
    o' my best ol' sorrel horse I'd raised, my hand clenched tangled mane.
Through the icy bubbles came a light that felt real warm,
    as it drew in closer a thousand wings encircled us in a swarm.
Ol' Sorrelly wasn't strugglin' much, it seemed he'd given up the fight,
    it was certain that ragin' river 'ould take the both of us that night.

The warm sun on my eyelids awoke me right at dawn,
    I jumped up to find the angels I had seen, but they were gone.
Ol' Sorrelly, he looked ragged 'n' he was actin' perty lame,
    he didn't seem to notice the branches hangin' in his mane.
It could o' been a dream I dreamed but that just don't construe,
    why me 'n' Sorrelly was sittin' there. Them wild angels must be true.

All I knew fer sure is we woke up on muddy banks,
    whoever'd helped us get there had gone to some great lengths.
An' ever' now 'n' then, although I know it sounds real strange,
    I see a flickerin' light at dusk amidst that Big Horn mountain range.
If ya ever travel through them parts pay attention to the breeze,
    I've heard them wild angels sing with the swayin' of the trees.

An' if ya ever chance to listen to a cowboy who says some things,
    'bout miracles in these parts er 'bout wild angel wings...
don't be too quick to judge him, listen closely to his tale,
    he's just another cowboy them wild angels saved from hell.

WINCHIN' SNORT

Well, Snort was one o' them horses that felt good beneath yer seat;
    roped both ends, spun a hole 'n' would drag it forty feet.
But Snort was kinda jumpy, well, I guess what I'm trying' to say,
    is groomin' wasn't somethin' Snort was up fer ever' day.
If yer thinkin' one could Ace him just a little now 'n' then,
    I'll tell ya a little secret: he don't let needles touch his skin.

It seems that ol' man Allister had been tippin' the bottle at night,
    an' dreamin' up a plan to make ol' Snort a desirable sight.
I'm sure ya can understand it was important he emphasize,
    the *talent* Snort displayed (despite the fly sores 'round his eyes.)
It always seemed to bother him when braggin' on his bay,
    that the horse he bred 'n' raised looked like an ol' ramuda stray.
His mane was rubbed out from the pipe, his tale was chewed up short,
    an' he just couldn't overlook the poop that matted up on Snort.

He really needed a shoein', cracked up toes 'n' long flat walls,
    but I couldn't get them farriers to return any o' my calls!
I suspect he had a tick, his left ear dropped down real low,
    but ever' time I tried to look, ol' Snort 'ould start to blow!
His coat was long 'n' coarse, them bumps were swellin big,
    no doubt that wormy horse was needin' an ivermectin swig!
Finally the word came down...ol' man Allister had a plan,
    but it was gonna require the efforts of more than one brave man.

Billy lured Snort into the haybarn with some grain,
    then laid the bucket down right in the center o' the lane.
In the center o' the lane a large canvas blanket lay,
    inconspicuously covered by some sprinklin's o' hay.
Connected to the canvas were four ropes so tightly bound,
    up over two bold rafters to two winches on the ground.

On the count o' three the winches switches all were tripped,
    suckin' Snort up off o' all four feet so he could then be flipped.
It required speedy work to get the ankle straps on tight,
    so Snort wouldn't wiggle outa them durin' the inevitable fight.
After placement o' the ankle straps securely 'round his feet,
    the winches' switches were released, Snort flipped over nice 'n' neat.

Snorts' cranky eyes were fixed in an evil, sulled up glare,
  as he dangled just a bit suspended ten feet in the air.

I must say the plan worked well, three silhouettes against the light;
  the Vet, the farrier 'n' the groom worked well into the night.
The farrier pounded shoes that clanged a rhythm that was seen,
  in the tappin' foot o' the Vet holdin' a thermometer that was green.
The buzzin' o' smokin' clippers could be heard a mile away,
  an' a haze o' smoke still lingered in the haybarn the next day.

Ol' man Allister reeks o' whiskey ever' time he tells the tale,
  o' the time we winched up Snort while munchin' grain out o' a pail.
There's a picture hangin' 'bove the fire of a big ol' fancy bay,
  a handsome horse that gleamed (at least he did for just one day).
An' if ya look real close ya'll notice his nostrils have a flare,
  an' in the background ya'll see a pile o' syringes, hooves 'n' hair!

There was a time, not too long ago, when some very gracious people did a very special thing for my husband Jimmie and I. We will never forget the warmth and support that we received at a very difficult time. This poem was written for those special people who bought raffle tickets for a mare that was donated for auction. The proceeds went to the Jimmie Paul Liver Transplant Fund. Thanks again to all of you who were so generous. We will always be grateful.

MISS THIRSTY CHEX

Yer carin' hearts reached out to help an ailin' friend,
    an' in return ya may just get a filly ya can tend.
A yearlin' that looks more like two, she's a perty sight,
    one of ya might be the one to own her late tonight.
Suppose she'll be a World Beater in her later years?
    Or will she be the beast from Hell that fulfills yer worst fears?

Might she be a rope horse, the kind ya'd never sell?
    Even fer a million bucks? Only time will tell!
She could be a halter horse, this one fact is clear.
    But what good is a halter horse if it won't rope a steer?

Would she be the kind ya'd brag about to all yer pals?
    Or would ya trade her off fer a good pair of romalls?
Think she'd like to gather cows on a big ole spread?
    Or rather crunch on oats in a fluffy sawdust bed?

Perhaps she'll be a Super Horse who'll do all the events!
    Lookin' at her daddy that possibility exists.
She might like her belly itched 'n' baths near ever' day.
    It's a bit too soon even fer an expert guy to say.

Ya know Christmas is a comin' if she eats ya out o' home,
    Salvation Army's always wantin' gifts fer those alone.
Ya may wanna hook her up to a cart and ride.
    (If ya make the cart real heavy it'll shorten up her stride.)

Ya may wanna race her and find a little guy,
    who calls himself a jockey. Ya might give that a try.
Or maybe ya could braid her mane with ribbons hangin' down,
    an' ride her with a flag when the rodeo comes to town!

Hey! Maybe ya could dress her up fer Halloween, of course!
   An' march her 'round the neighborhood as a scary, monster horse.

Then again, ya may just wanna put her in a stall,
   feed her hay 'n' water 'til she grows fat 'n' tall.
By then ya may decide to let an expert try her out,
   but there are many trainers in Cave Creek 'n' about.

I would say the closest barn (if Squire's place is full),
   is just around the corner 'n' he doesn't dish ya bull.
He'll likely treat ya right since ya own the very mare,
   that helped him buy a liver 'n' get the best o' care.

No matter what ya do with her or what she does become,
   remember she's a special horse cuz she helped the man I love.

Jim Paul on Bonita San in 1979.

ABOUT THE ILLUSTRATOR

JIM PAUL, SR.

Born in 1937 in Sacramento, California, Jim was one of four children. He was born with a wealth of artistic talent that has emerged in every aspect of his life. His obvious knack with western illustrations is just one example of his tremendous talent. As a successful performance horse trainer he has enhanced his training program with bits, spurs, hackamore bits, tie downs and other tack that were originally designed to meet specific needs he had, however, he finds himself busy building items for friends and referrals who have heard of his outstanding work. Some of his bits have sold for over $500.00. His artistic creations are too vast to mention, including ironworks for hat racks, halter racks as well as barbed wire sculptures.

He and his first wife Betty raised three boys, two of which are also successful performance horse trainers. Randy and Jimmie combined have trained many Champions in reining, working cowhorse and roping events. Their youngest son, John, followed his love for music. As a drummer, he writes songs and has formed his own band. All three have inherited Jim's love for a twelve string guitar. One of Jim's favorite past times is to pick at guitars with his sons.

In the 70's Jim was the model and spokesperson for Dan Post boots. Through the years of training performance horses Jim has trained such legendary horses as Bull Parker and Skeeto. His outstanding reputation as a horseman has allowed him to hold many judging cards, two of which, NCHA (National Cutting Horse Association) and AQHA (American Quarter Horse Association), he has held for over thirty years.

Jim continues to train performance horses in Cave Creek, Arizona where he lives with his wife, Dema. He shares a training facility with his son Jimmie and his daughter-in-law, the author, Lisa.

Left to Right: **the Paul's Jimmie, Lane, Will, Lisa, Lex Ote and Skunk.**

ABOUT THE AUTHOR

I can't remember a time that we didn't have horses when I was growing up. In fact, I thought everyone had horses! (Of course, everyone we knew did.) The youngest of three children, I was born in Phoenix and raised up in the pines of Prescott, Arizona. I spent many hours baking mud pies with grass sprinkles at horse shows (no telling what the mud was made of) and started showing horses at the tender age of four. My first pony, a paint shetland named Belle Star, won me few blue ribbons but supplied hearty entertainment for the crowds! And looking back on home movies, Belle Star taught me to ride...I mean *really* ride! I went on to show Quarter Horses successfully in trail and western pleasure and eventually reining and working cowhorse.

My personal goals in performance events, such as roping and working cowhorse, play second fiddle to our performance horse business and our two sons, Lex and Lane. My husband Jimmie, the trainer of many World Champion and Reserve World Champion horses, is a strong, quiet, yet stubborn cowboy that many accuse of being born one hundred years after his time! Through Jimmie's stories and those of many special people, I've been inspired.

Over time I've been blessed to meet many legends in the horse and rodeo industries. And I've never passed up a good story from the heart of an "Old Timer". Around the fire on special nights the guitars of my husband, his brothers and my father-in-law play in harmony as my boys look on. They learn about a cowboy's life back in another time by listening to the old western songs their grandpa loves to sing. The branches in my family tree support Professional Rodeo Cowboys, ranchers, dog trainers, horse trainers and champions in the making. The tales of these special people are forever branded on my mind. Their experiences, and mine, are relived in the words of my poetry. And I hope someday, far from now, I'll be one of the "Old Timers" that young ears stop to listen to.

Lisa Paul.

GLOSSARY

The definitions listed in this glossary relate to the poems in The Cowboy
Way and are defined as simply as possible.

A Hand: A person who has a talent for understanding and riding horses.

Baldy: A horse that has a white face that extends behind one or both eyes
and covers the nose.

Bay: A horse color ranging from light yellow to a dark red and always has
a black mane and tail.

Box: A somewhat confined area on either side of a chute used for roping
cattle. This area is where the horse and rider wait to rope the stock
coming out of the chute.

Bridle Path: A shaved area of mane beginning behind the forelock and
traveling back anywhere from one inch to six or eight inches.

Bute: Short name for Phenylbutazone or Butazoladine. An
anti-inflammatory agent frequently used on horses.

Coils: The extra length of a rope that is held in a circular pattern in one
hand while the other hand swings the loop used to catch.

Crocodile: A famous jumping horse.

Curb: A thickening or "bowing" of a specific ligament due to strain.

Dally: The wrapping of a rope around a horn or post, etc. to stop it from
sliding.

Flank Strap: A strap placed tight around the flank of a horse, used to
encourage the horse to buck.

Forelock: A lock of mane that grows between the ears down toward the
eye.

Gelding: A stallion that has been "castrated".

Girth: The area of the horse behind the shoulders and under the belly
where the cinch of a saddle goes.

Go: A "turn" at a rodeo, horse show or other equine event.

Header: The first partner in team roping. The header ropes the "head" of
of the steer.

Heeler: The second partner in team roping. The heeler ropes the "heels"
or ankles of the steer.

Hock: The joint between the cannon bone and the fibula on the hind leg
of many animals. It resembles an elbow.

Hock Hobbles: A training device with a long rein and strap that is attached
to the hock and then attached to a bit.

GLOSSARY

Ivermectin: A medicine to treat worms.

Leather New: A product sprayed on leather to make it supple.

Mark: The act of placing both spurs forward of the shoulder when broncs or bulls break out of the chute. Mandatory in order to receive a score in rodeo.

Navicular: A degenerative disease in the hoof that is usually seen in older horses, but not always.

Rasp: A tool used by horse shoers to file the hoof.

Riggin: A "handle" for bareback bronc riders to hold on to.

Roached Mane: A mane that has been shaved as to leave no hair showing, only stubble.

Roan: A horse color that has white hairs intermingled with one or more basic colors. These horses often look "soapy".

Show Sheen: A product used on manes and tails to make them shine.

Side Bone: A disease found most frequently in the front feet of horses. Commonly seen in heavier horses and/or horses used for strenuous activity such as team roping and jumping.

Slack: The space between the rope dallied at the saddle horn and the end where the loop is.

Socks: White markings that cover the entire leg up to, and often covering, the knee.

Sorrel: A horse color that is some shade of red and always has a red mane and tail.

Suicide Wrap: A way of wrapping a bull rope around a cowboy's hand that doesn't allow it to release as easily as other wraps.

The Well: An area on the outside of an animal's neck that is a common place for a person riding to get pulled in to when an animal moves quickly left, right or back.

Withers: An area on the backbone where the body joins the neck.

Wood: A saddle.

ORDER FORM

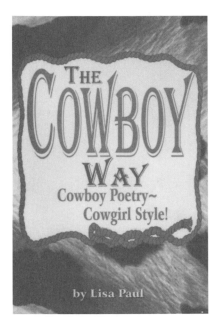

Once there was a pony who had read
some fantastic tales, 'bout some
cowpokes and their ponies along
some dusty trails.

This pony told another 'bout the
good stuff he had read,
"It's *The Cowboy Way* by Lisa Paul",
is what that pony said.

Soon the word spread fast through
herds of ponies everywhere,
and book orders for *The Cowboy
Way* poured in from far and near.

It's assumed that every pony has
read The Cowboy Way by now,
but if you come across a cranky one,
please get him one…here's how:

MAIL TO:
LISA PAUL
4125 E. PINNACLE VISTA DR.
CAVE CREEK AZ 85331

**SEND MONEY ORDER, PERSONAL, OR CASHIERS CHECK
(U.S. FUNDS ONLY) PAYABLE TO: LISA PAUL**

- -

(Please Print Only)

_____ **BOOKS ORDERED**
X $12.95 EACH = _____

DATE ____ / ____ / ____

S/H $3.00 PER ORDER _____

Thank You for your Order!

TOTAL AMOUNT ENCLOSED $ _____

SHIP TO:

NAME _____ **COMPANY** _____

ADDRESS _____

CITY _____ **STATE** _____ **ZIP** _____

PHONE (   ) _____ **FAX (   )** _____